BARBARA JUSTER ESBENSEN

WHO SHRANK MY GRANDMOTHER'S HOUSE?

POEMS OF DISCOVERY

PICTURES BY ERIC BEDDOWS

Douglas & McIntyre
Vancouver/Toronto

Also by Barbara Juster Esbensen:

COLD STARS AND FIREFLIES
Poems of the Four Seasons

WORDS WITH WRINKLED KNEES
Animal Poems

Published in Canada by Douglas & McIntyre 1992
First published in the United States by HarperCollins Publishers 1992

Text copyright © 1992 by Barbara Juster Esbensen
Illustrations copyright © 1992 by Eric Beddows

Douglas & McIntyre Ltd.
585 Bloor Street West
Toronto, Ontario M6G 1K5

Canadian Cataloguing in Publication Data

Esbensen, Barbara Juster
    Who shrank my grandmother's house?

ISBN 1-55054-211-7

1. Children's poetry, American.   I. Beddows, Eric,
1951– .   II. Title.

PS3555.S24W4 1992   811'.54   C91-095264-7

Contents

Author's Note

Each of these poems is about a discovery. Each poem reminds you that every day, and all around you, there are discoveries to be made. The most ordinary things can suddenly seem new and unexpected. A pencil can give up an astonishing secret without any help from us. A door becomes a living thing with a personality all its own. In a darkening city park, the fountains wear ghostly veils.

Day after day, we discover our own lives. Because we never know what we will find, every discovery is an unexpected gift we give to ourselves. We open it and something new is revealed. A secret is uncovered.

As you wander among these poems, you will make discoveries of your own. Letters and words are already arranging themselves into unexpected ideas and images on every page.

You are the discoverer. The poems are waiting.

—Barbara J. Esbensen

Pencils

The rooms in a pencil
are narrow
but elephants   castles and watermelons
fit in

In a pencil
noisy words yell for attention
and quiet words wait their turn

How did they slip
into such a tight place?
Who
gives them their
lunch?

From a broken pencil
an unbroken poem will come!
There is a long story living
in the shortest pencil

Every word in your
pencil
is fearless   ready to walk
the blue tightrope lines
Ready
to teeter and smile
down   Ready to come right out
and show you
thinking!

Clouds

Don't trust the wind
The wind
is making these maps
Don't look for your street
on these maps   Whole cities
dissolve
Their buildings
swirl
out of sight

Don't count on the wind
The wind
is drawing these maps
chalking them in
with one hand   wiping them
out
with the other!

11

Doors

Some doors
are always open   Some
doors hold themselves
shut
The open doors say
"Come on in" and
"I missed you"
and
"Have a sandwich"
The closed doors
just shake their heads

I know a door
that collects things
collects
leaves   scratches
chipped paint
parts of words
It is an old door
getting gray and crabby
The other day
it said "SLAM!!"   and collected
my fingers

Geode

I crack the stone egg

Here is a city   frozen
in a hollow
stone

Who walks the halls
of these chiseled towers?
What voices echo
in the vaulted glass rooms?

Listen
to
the busy sound
of crystal traffic   thin as a splinter

The sharp-shadowed
sun
rises and sets   transparent
in this amethyst sky

Time

Until we invented clocks
we counted the hours
in sunlight
and shadow   On cloudy days
everybody came in late   or
early   Everybody
apologized   to
everybody   There was
no order in the cave

Now clocks inch past
YESTERDAY   Clocks hammer away
at TODAY
For a clock TOMORROW
looks just like the day
before

Until we invented
tick
and tock
we watched the pendulum-moon
swing in the night sky
marking star-seconds
blink! blink! blink!

The Rescue

Rain poured down   The house
rocked and bucked   like a ship
towed through the dark
with long ropes of rain

We hauled her in   awash on the deck
tossed up
like a fish   from the bottom
of the lawn   drenched
in blue light

Warm now
in the kitchen's safe harbor
she tumbles in yarn
but lightning still clings
to her paw   a small
thunder
alive in her chest!
What shall we call her?

Storm Cat!

Old Photograph Album:
Grandfather

I see him one Christmas
in his leather
aviator hat   the flaps
buckled under his
chin   His hand
is holding the rope
of the Flexible Flyer sled
You can tell it is made of wood

It is piled with Christmas presents
all wrapped in black
and white and gray   A black tree
trimmed with fat white
lights
stands on the porch

The skies of his childhood
are gray   Here he is
in his swimming
suit and his waterwings
He is squinting at the gray sun
that blazes down
on small black sailboats   white
sails   and on the gray waves
lapping at the sand

He is a gray child   and his big dog
is dark gray   Even his baby sister
is gray   Her white curls
bob in the wind   and a gray robin
hops
   off the page

Summer Night: Canoeing

The rising moon pulls
this paper boat   this folded leaf
that carries me
on the water
along the brightening path

I am paper too   white edged
casting no shadow
on the water   weightless
as a moth

In the moonlight
leaves   like shaken mirrors
reflect a fish-scale moon
rocking   rocking
on the water   silver
brushed with blue

Sparrow Dreaming

When morning comes
the sky
will pour itself through
blue doors

The wind will rush in—
its blue scarves like
sails

Behind the sun
the blue silk of the wind
will flutter and fold

When morning comes
even the wing of the dullest
bird
will be edged
with blue!

Four Poems for Roy G Biv

Roy G Biv is not a real person at all. These letters look like someone's name, but actually they are a good way for you to remember the arrangement of the colors you see in prism light or a rainbow: red—orange—yellow—green—blue—indigo—violet!

Prism in the Window

I wake to light
falling through glass
colors splintering and clashing
in the air

The noise of morning sunlight
being smashed apart
wakes me

This is my alarm!

Color falls on color
I hear cymbal sound
breaking into rainbow dust
shattering
into seven
rainbow chimes!

PRISM!

A Question

If I shine
a white bird
through my biggest prism
will it break into
one cardinal   one
bluebird and five
parakeets?

Rainbow Making

1. A Mystery

How can it be
that a stick
tipped
   with grease
   from
   somebody's old
   Buick
   will flare
   rainbow tails
when you float it
on any puddle
in this world—sun
or no sun?

Rainbow Making

2. Magic

Turn on the hose
and a rainbow will come
fighting your thumb
numb
on the nozzle

A rainbow
will flash
in the fan of cold
spray

Imagine!

A rainbow fan
painted
in sunlight and spray
opening   closing
shimmering
under your own
cold
thumb!

Sand Dollar

What can we buy
with this loose
money?

It spilled
from the green silk
pocket
of the sea
a white coin tossed up
a careless gift   wet
shining
at the water's edge

Who can break a dollar?

What a bargain! Five
white doves
ready to fly to your hand

Sea change!

The sand dollar is an animal that lives in
warm coastal waters. Its shell is a thin, flat
circle. If you break open this shell, you can
shake out five white "doves." When the animal
was alive, these dove-shaped pieces were the
animal's teeth.

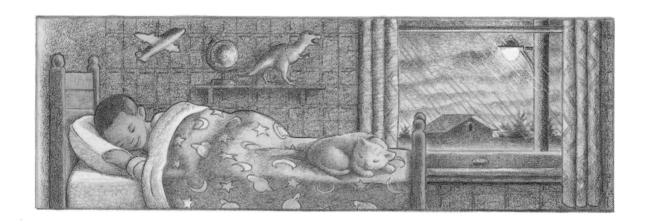

Lullaby for a Rainy Night

Soon you will be
asleep
Windy fingers will move
over and over your house
and wash
the faces of streetlights
with rain

Listen!   The cars
go by   Their tires
unzip the wet streets   Their
lights
stroke the ceiling
with yellow hands

Soon you will fall
asleep
to the sound of rain
leaning
into slick shadows
under the cars—
to the sound of rain
moving slow fingers
on the roof

Sunrise

All night
I traveled the shadowed roads
behind my eyes   I lived
in mysterious vanished
rooms
I called out
the names of strangers   lost
my way

Now the sleepy clock downstairs
wakens   stretches its hands
to the metal sun
red half dome
gonging its way up
from the cage of black trees
antennas
and sharp roofs
outside my window

I am home

Homework

It rustles   it
shifts   with no wind
in the room to
move it
Listen!
The blank white
paper
needs your attention

"Where are the words?"
it whispers
"I'm lonesome
for words and circles
and
spelling your name and
assignments"

Put your hand on the paper
to calm it   Pick up
your pen   Say
"Paper   I'm here
when you need me!"

Begin

My Cat

My cat is asleep—white paws
folded under
his chin   He is a soft gray
smudge on the round rug

Dozing in the sun
He is a warm round stone
with a fur collar

My cat is taking
a nap   Not a whisker
trembles   Not a hair
moves   His breath goes
softly in and out

Stay in your holes
mice!   My cat sees you
in his dreams
and he has left
his motor running!

Tell Me

Why do you think
the birches
tore off their yellow
sweaters
on the windiest coldest day
of all   waved good-bye
and watched them scatter
down the street?

Why do you think
the birches
are standing in our yard
in their underwear?

Friends

I am drawing a picture
My house is in it
A jagged yellow sun
hangs from the blue strip
of sky   I am drawing
a dog   His tail is wagging
He wants to be
my dog

I am drawing
the sound of a train far off
I will   scribble in
some smoke   I might want to
travel

Your house is in my picture
It is leaning across our street
I am putting the word POW!
and electric zigzags
where our chimneys
almost touch

In this picture
I am waving from my window   You
are running up our walk
A bird is flying off the edge
of the page   singing
Anything can happen
in pictures

I don't
need to draw our faces
We will never forget
each other

In Autumn

For H.K.D.

I am the astronomer of
orchards
I know the secrets
hidden there

(Macintosh   Winesap   Cortland
Winter Permain)

Every apple is a
universe
In every slice
a secret star!

(Rome Beauty   Gravenstein
Golden Delicious)

I am the astronomer of orchards
I am
the discoverer   the splitter
of apples   You must call me
Star finder!

(Bellflower   Spitzbergen
Northern Spy)

*Find out for yourself what happens when you
lay an apple on its side and cut it in half.*

Nightfall

One by one
that dark magician
Night
folds the colors of the day
like scarves
and hides them
in his sleeves

We run
holding our balloons
of no color
We run through the park
and the dark grass
grows shadows of
deeper dark   In the flower beds
every flower
is gray   The fountain
is a drifting ghost

Night
that dark magician
is racing us home
stopping only to turn off
the merry-go-round
with its little black horses
blockprinted
on the empty scene

The Visit

Who
shrank my grandmother's
house?   I mean
the banister
is cut off at
the knees!   Last year
I had to stretch
to slide my hands along
the rail   hauling myself
up
step-by-step-by-step

In every room
the walls move in
to take a closer
look   "My!" they whisper
corner to corner
(The curtains
hold their breath)
"How you have grown!"